Mercy Watson Thinks Like a Pig

Kate DiCamillo

Mercy Watson

Thinks Like a Pig

illustrated by Chris Van Dusen

CANDLEWICK PRESS
CAMBRIDGE, MASSACHUSETTS

Text copyright © 2008 by Kate DiCamillo
Illustrations copyright © 2008 by Chris Van Dusen

First edition 2008

Library of Congress Cataloging-in-Publication Data

DiCamillo, Kate.
Mercy Watson thinks like a pig / Kate DiCamillo ;
illustrated by Chris Van Dusen. — 1st ed.
p.   cm.
Summary: After Mercy Watson follows the delightful scent
and delicious taste of the pansies her thoughtful neighbors plant
to beautify their yard, Animal Control Officer Francine Poulet
is called out to handle the case, which brings unexpected results.
ISBN 978-0-7636-3265-6
[1. Pigs—Fiction. 2. Flowers—Fiction. 3. Humorous stories.]
I. Van Dusen, Chris, ill. II. Title.
PZ7.D5455Mt 2008
[Fic]—dc22   2007040623

2 4 6 8 10 9 7 5 3 1

Printed in China

This book was typeset in Mrs. Eaves.
The illustrations were done in gouache.

Candlewick Press
2067 Massachusetts Avenue
Cambridge, Massachusetts 02140

visit us at www.candlewick.com

For Chris Van Dusen,
who is the best pig-thinker of them all

K. D.

For Carolyn, the sister I never had

C. V.

Chapter
1

Mr. Watson and Mrs. Watson have a pig named Mercy.

Mr. Watson, Mrs. Watson, and Mercy live together in a house at 54 Deckawoo Drive.

One day, Mr. Watson and Mrs. Watson and Mercy were sitting on their patio.

Mr. Watson and Mrs. Watson and Mercy were drinking lemonade.

Mr. Watson said, "Mrs. Watson, this lemonade makes my lips feel puckery."

"I put an awful lot of lemons in it," said Mrs. Watson.

"That explains it," said Mr. Watson.

Mercy slurped some lemonade from her bowl.

"Isn't it a beautiful day?" said Mrs. Watson.

"Absolutely beautiful," said Mr. Watson.

Mercy grunted.

Chapter

Next door to the Watsons, Baby Lincoln and Eugenia Lincoln were standing in their front yard.

"Baby," said Eugenia, "we live next door to a pig."

"Yes, Sister," said Baby, "we do."
"But that does not stop us from living a gracious life," said Eugenia.
"It doesn't?" said Baby.

Eugenia handed Baby a shovel.

"What's this for?" said Baby.

"We are going to beautify our yard," Eugenia said. "We are going to plant pansies. You, Baby, will dig. And I, Eugenia, will plant."

"Yes, Sister," said Baby.

"We will lead a gracious life even if it kills us," said Eugenia Lincoln.

"Yes, Sister."

Baby sighed.

She began to dig.

Chapter
3

On the Watsons' patio, Mercy put her snout up in the air.

She sniffed.

There was a delightful smell coming from next door.

Mercy pushed her snout through the hedge.

She looked into the Lincoln
Sisters' yard.

She saw Eugenia Lincoln put a
flower in the ground.

What was going on?

Mercy waited until Eugenia disappeared around the corner.

She pushed through the hedge and trotted into the Lincoln Sisters' yard.

She sniffed the flower that Eugenia had planted.

The flower smelled delicious.

Mercy took a bite.

It tasted delicious, too.

Chapter
4

On the other side of the house, Eugenia Lincoln planted her last pansy.

"There," said Eugenia. "It looks spectacular, doesn't it?"

"It does," said Baby.

"I believe I will go around front and admire the overall effect," said Eugenia.

Eugenia Lincoln went around front.

Mercy burped.

She moved on to flower number three.

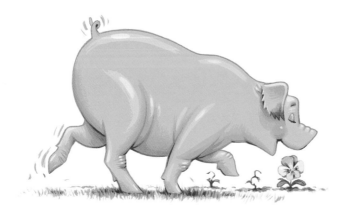

When she had eaten the whole
flower, she looked up and saw
another flower.

She ate that one, too.

But there was no overall effect to
admire.

"BABY!" screamed Eugenia.

"Yes, Sister?" said Baby.

"Where have all the flowers gone?"
shouted Eugenia.

"Oh, dear," said Baby. "They were
here just a minute ago."

Mercy came around the corner.

There was a spring in her step.

There were pansy petals on her chin.

"PIG!" shouted Eugenia.
"Pig, pig, pig!"
Eugenia Lincoln ran toward Mercy.

Mercy kicked up her heels.

She ran away from Eugenia.

Chapter
5

Meanwhile, back on the Watsons' patio, the Watsons were wondering where Mercy had gone.

"She was here just a minute ago," said Mrs. Watson.

"She can't have gone far," said Mr. Watson.

Mr. Watson and Mrs. Watson went looking for Mercy.

"Oh," said Mrs. Watson, "there she is. And look, she's playing a game of tag with Eugenia. They look so happy."

"I don't think that Sister is playing," said Baby. "And I don't think that Sister is happy."

"She's not?" said Mr. Watson

"No," said Baby, "she's not. Mercy ate every one of Sister's pansies."

"She must be hungry,"said Mrs. Watson. "Mercy!" Mrs. Watson called. "Come inside and have a little toast with a great deal of butter on it."

Mercy came running.

She came running quickly.

Mercy loved toast.

She particularly loved toast with a great deal of butter on it.

Chapter
6

Baby Lincoln was correct.

Eugenia Lincoln was not happy.

"I have had it," said Eugenia. "I have been pushed too far."

"Oh, dear," said Baby.

"I am ready to take extreme measures," said Eugenia Lincoln.

"Extreme measures?" said Baby.

"I am calling Animal Control,"
said Eugenia.

"Oh, Sister, no," said Baby.

"Oh, Sister, yes," said Eugenia.

She got out the phone book.

She ran her finger down the page.

"Please, Sister," said Baby.

Eugenia stabbed a number with her finger.

"Here we go," she said.

"Oh, Sister, please think about what you are doing," said Baby.

"I know exactly what I am doing," said Eugenia. "I am kissing that pig good-bye."

Chapter
7

The phone rang at the Animal Control Center.

Animal Control Officer Francine Poulet answered.

"Help you?" said Francine Poulet.

"Yes," said the voice on the other end of the line. "I am calling to report an animal desperately in need of control."

"Got yourself a rabid dog?" said Francine.

"Well, no," said the voice on the other end.

"Stray cat?"

"Certainly not," said the voice.

"Raccoon in your trash?"

"No."

"Squirrel in your chimney?"

"I think not."

"Snake in your toilet?"

"I beg your pardon!"

"Let me think," said Francine Poulet. "It's not a dog or a cat. It's not a raccoon or a squirrel. And it's definitely not a snake. What could it be? Wait a minute," said Francine. "You're not dealing with a skunk, are you?"

"What I'm dealing with is a pig!"

"A pig?"

"A pig!"

"Give me the address," said Francine Poulet.

"Fifty-four Deckawoo Drive," said the voice.

33

Chapter
8

At 54 Deckawoo Drive, Mercy was on the couch taking an after-toast nap.

She was snoring.

"What a peaceful afternoon," said Mrs. Watson.

"Indeed," said Mr. Watson.

Knock, knock, knock.

"Someone is at the back door," said Mrs. Watson.

"I'll get it," said Mr. Watson. He went into the kitchen.

"Come in, Baby," said Mr. Watson.

"I can't," said Baby. "Something terrible is going to happen."

"It is?"

"An unmentionable horror approaches."

"It does?"

"Oh, Mr. Watson," said Baby Lincoln, "you must protect her."

"Protect her?" said Mr. Watson. "Protect who?"

Baby threw herself into Mr. Watson's arms. She began to cry.

"There, there," said Mr. Watson.

Mrs. Watson came into the kitchen. "What is going on?" she said.

"It seems an Unmentionable Horror is approaching," said Mr. Watson.

"Oh, dear," said Mrs. Watson.
"I have always been terribly afraid of
Unmentionable Horrors. What will
we do?"

"There, there," said Mr. Watson.
"I am sure we will think of something."

Chapter
9

Mercy was still on the living-room couch.

KNOCK, KNOCK, KNOCK.

She opened one eye.

KNOCK, KNOCK, KNOCK.

Mercy opened both eyes.

The Watsons' front door swung open.

"Mercy," said Stella, "we are having a tea party and you are invited."

Mercy yawned.

"I don't think she's interested," said Frank.

"There will be big pieces of cake and cream puffs and cheese toast," said Stella.

Mercy sat up.

Actually, she was interested.

"There will be éclairs and pancakes and enchiladas," said Stella.

Mercy was very interested.

"But," said Stella, "if you come to the tea party, you have to wear a hat. Everybody at a proper tea party wears a hat."

Mercy thought about hats.

She thought about food.

She got off the couch.

She followed Frank and Stella out
the front door.

Chapter
10

Animal Control Officer Francine Poulet was on her way to 54 Deckawoo Drive.

"Francine," she said to herself, "you've never encountered a pig before. This is a career-expanding opportunity."

At the corner of Creek and
Windingo, Francine spotted a dog.
She stopped the truck.

"Hello, little friend," said
Francine Poulet. "Are you lost?"
"Erf?" said the dog.
"Just as I suspected," said
Francine. "No tags. Hop in!"

On Merkle Street, a golden retriever stepped right in front of Animal Control Officer Francine Poulet's truck. "Tsk, tsk," said Francine Poulet. "Foolish dog."

She stopped the truck.

She got out.

"Quick like a bunny," said Francine Poulet to the golden retriever.

The golden retriever hopped in.

"Francine," said Francine Poulet, "you are the best Animal Control Officer in the history of animal control. Nothing can stop you. Not even a pig!"

Chapter
11

By the time Francine Poulet turned onto Deckawoo Drive, her truck was full of dogs.

"To catch a pig," said Francine, "what I need to do is think like a pig."

The dogs in the back of the truck howled.

"Think like a pig, think like a pig," said Francine Poulet.

She saw a man and a woman running down the street.

"Excuse me," said Francine, "have you seen a pig?"

"We have lost her!" said the woman.

"Lost who?" said Francine.

"Mercy," said the man. "Our darling, our dear. She is in great danger."

"An Unmentionable Horror
approaches," said the woman.

"An Unmentionable Horror?"
said Francine Poulet.

"Exactly!" said the man.

"All righty, then," said Francine.
"Thank you very much."

She rolled up her window.

"You are on your own here, Francine," said Francine Poulet. "The locals are as crazy as loons."

The dogs in the back of the truck barked and growled.

"I know, I know," Francine told them. "Think like a pig."

Chapter 12

Mercy was wearing a hat.

She was watching Stella pour imaginary tea.

She was watching Stella slice imaginary cake.

Mercy was not having a good time.

Where were the enchiladas and
cream puffs?

Mercy's stomach growled.

Where were the pancakes and éclairs?

"Would you like some more?" said
Stella.

Some more of what? Mercy wondered.
She snorted.

"Isn't this lovely?" said Stella.

"I don't think Mercy is happy,"
said Frank.

"Everybody is always happy at a tea party," said Stella.

"I'm not happy," said Frank. "I'm hungry. Plus, I look stupid in this hat."

"Oh, please," said Stella. "Here, have some more cake."

Chapter
13

Animal Control Officer Francine
Poulet was scouting the backyards of
Deckawoo Drive.

She leaped over hedges.

She crept through flower beds.

She thought piggy thoughts.

She climbed a tree and surveyed
the yard below her.

She saw three people wearing hats.

She saw three people sitting at a
table having tea.

"Isn't that nice?" said Francine
Poulet. "Isn't that sweet?"

Francine looked more closely.

"Wait a minute," she said. "One of those people is not a person. One of those people is a pig! Francine, you have located the pig. You are the best Animal Control Officer in the history of the world! And now you must capture the pig. On the count of three. One. Two."

Francine Poulet closed her eyes.

She leaped from the tree.

"THREEEEEEEEEE!"

Chapter
14

Mercy decided that she had had more than enough of nothing.

She stood up.

She was going home.

Suddenly, there was a high-pitched yell.

A woman fell from the sky and landed headfirst on the tea table.

Stella screamed.

Frank screamed
louder.

Mercy screamed
loudest of all.

One street over, Mr. Watson said to Mrs. Watson, "Do you hear what I hear?"

"That is our darling," said Mrs. Watson. "That is our dear. And she is in trouble."

Mr. Watson and Mrs. Watson started to run.

Chapter
15

Animal Control Officer Francine
Poulet rolled off the table.

She wrapped her arms around Mercy.

"Think . . . like . . . a . . . pig?" said
Francine.

Mr. Watson and Mrs. Watson came
running into the backyard.

"You found her!" said Mrs. Watson.

"You are our hero!" said Mr. Watson.

"You landed right directly on top of your head!" said Frank.

"I do feel a little woozy," said Francine.

"Maybe you're just hungry," said Mrs. Watson. "Maybe you need some toast."

"Toast?" said Francine.

Toast, thought Mercy.

"These dogs look hungry, too," said Mrs. Watson. "Would you fellows like some toast?"

"I wonder if this is a good idea," said Francine Poulet as she let the dogs out of the truck.

"It's a wonderful idea," said Mrs. Watson. "Now, Stella, run next door and invite Eugenia and Baby to our small celebration."

"Tell them it is in honor of . . ." Mr. Watson turned to Francine. "What is your name, my dear?"

"My name is Animal Control Officer Francine Poulet," said Francine, "and I've been trying to think like a pig."

"Well," said Mr. Watson, "not just anybody can think like a pig. Not just anybody can be a porcine wonder."

"I guess not," said Francine.

"You keep trying, dear," said Mrs. Watson. "In the meantime, let's all go have some toast!"

Kate DiCamillo is the author of *The Miraculous Journey of Edward Tulane*; *The Tale of Despereaux*, which received the Newbery Medal; *The Tiger Rising*, which was named a National Book Award Finalist; and *Because of Winn-Dixie*, which received a Newbery Honor. She says, "I take absolutely no credit for this book. If you laugh as you read about the exploits of Mercy Watson and Animal Control Officer Francine Poulet, it is entirely due to the genius of Chris Van Dusen. Writing about Mercy, imagining the wacky people who enter her orbit, and then standing back and watching Chris bring them all to glorious, hilarious life . . . that has to be the best job on the planet. Thank you, Mr. Van Dusen." Kate DiCamillo lives in Minnesota.

Chris Van Dusen is the author-illustrator of *Down to the Sea with Mr. Magee*, *A Camping Spree with Mr. Magee*, and *If I Built a Car*. He says, "In each book, Kate adds a new person to the cast of characters. Here, it's Francine Poulet, and she's great! It's my job to develop them visually, and I start by looking for clues in the name. In this case, Francine Poulet HAD to look like a chicken! I've never drawn a person with a nose like Francine's, but every chicken needs a beak!" Chris Van Dusen lives in Maine.